My Birthmark,

My Gift

Chibuzor Mirian Azubuike

My Birthmark, My Gift

© Chibuzor Mirian Azubuike 2020

ISBN: 978-978-984-163-9

chibuzorazubuike.com

hello@chibuzorazubuike.com

+2348061258783

Instagram : chibuzor_azubuike

Printed in Nigeria

DEDICATION

This book is dedicated to my lovely daughter, Nchedo. Your birthmarks are marks of uniqueness and badges of honour. Wear them with grace. Grow in confidence, you are unstoppable. I love you, dear child.

CHAPTER ONE

THE BIRTH OF CHEDO

In Nigeria, a country in Africa, a girl was born with a birthmark, her name was Chedo. Her mother, Chizoba, gave birth to her after 24 hours of intense labour and pain, and when she saw her beautiful daughter, she smiled so joyfully that her baby, who was laid in her cot, began to smile too.

Chedo's eyes were closed while she laughed with her mother, this made her mother wonder if Chedo could see her.

"Nurse Chika, can my baby see? How does she know that I am smiling?" Chizoba asked with an astonishing look on her face.

"Well, babies can't see until they are three weeks old, but don't be surprised, ma'am, she may not see you yet, but the bond between mothers and their children is so strong, so yes, she can feel you are happy to finally meet her. With time, she will get to know you, through your smell."

They both chuckled.

Chizoba regained her strength after resting for about an hour. The nurses brought her baby close to her so that baby could latch on well. She was told this would improve the mother to daughter bond and her baby would feel safe outside, after being in her mother's womb for nine months. When Chedo was placed on her mother's bosom and Chizoba took a closer look at her baby, she found out that she had a big birthmark on her right arm. It was so large that it extended from her elbow to her wrist.

"What is this big black thing on my daughter's arm?" Chizoba asked one of the nurses.

"It is called the Mongolian spot and it is common among babies with dark skin.

Chizoba felt that the mark made her daughter even more special and she vowed to raise a confident child.

When they got home, Nonso, her husband, said, "Let us celebrate and be thankful for this time. Let us take pictures and make good memories so that when things become bad, we would hold on to such beautiful memories."

Nonso said he was so happy to be a father and could not stop looking at his beautiful beloved daughter.

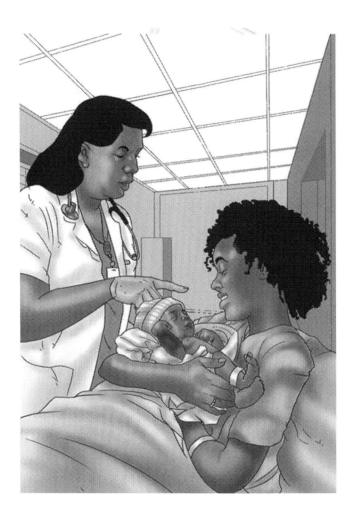

CHAPTER TWO

BULLYING AT SCHOOL

C hedo grew up so fast, a pretty seven year old girl, who loved herself and was kind to others. She was a brilliant artist and her friends and teachers were proud to be associated with her. This made Eka, her classmate, envious of her.

"Chedo is so proud. Does she think she is the only one that can draw? I would look for a part of her that she does not like so that I can make jest of her." Eka vowed to her friends.

One day, Chedo went to the tap behind the class to wash her hands. Coincidentally, Eka was there when Chedo turned on the tap. Eka, spoiling for a fight, went to turn it off and the two girls began to struggle. As they struggled with the tap, Chedo's sleeves rolled up her arms and Eka saw her birthmark and told her rudely, "Your hands are already ugly, why are you trying to wash it? Even if you wash it from today till next year, they would remain that way!"

Immediately she said this, the other girls drew closer to Chedo to see her hand and they laughed as they listened to Eka mock Chedo.

Chedo felt so bad, she wished she could disappear and none of the jeering girls would see her any more.

She cried as she walked away. She did not say a lot as the laughter from the other girls was too loud and no one would have heard her even if she spoke. She wished she had a beautiful hand like Eka. Eka's hands were so beautiful because her body and her hands had the same complexion, Chedo thought.

She walked straight to their teacher and told her what just happened. The teacher sent for Eka immediately.

"Eka, why did you call Chedo's hand ugly?" their teacher, Mrs Mary, asked.

"She is lying, I did not say that," Eka answered, looking away from Chedo.

"You said so," Chedo replied, as tears dropped from her eyes.

"I did not," Eka insisted.

Eka continued to deny it and their teacher became more confused, she did not know which of the girls was telling the truth.

"Who was there when it happened?" Mrs Mary asked.

"Dera and Titi were present." Chedo replied. She was happy that finally, the girls will say the truth and their teacher would believe her.

"Dera and Titi, since you both are witnesses when the event happened, I want to hear the truth. Did Eka ever call Chedo's hand ugly?" Mrs Mary asked.

"No ma, Eka never said that," they chorused, looking at their friend, Eka, who had earlier given them a sign to support her.

Mrs Mary did not see Eka signaling the girls to lie, so she told Eka and Chedo to apologise to each other for fighting.

This only made Chedo sadder because she did nothing wrong. Eka continued to mock Chedo's birthmark and even when Chedo said she would report to their teacher, Eka laughed and said no one would believe her.

Chedo never knew there was anything wrong with her birthmark or even her hands, until Eka started mocking her.

Chedo's best friend, Kay, continued to encourage Chedo to ignore Eka and instead, focus on the upcoming State Drawing Competition. But Chedo was still disturbed because Eka was mean to her. Chedo and Kay were best of friends; they loved each other so much and shared the same birth date, so they always marked their birthday celebration together.

CHAPTER THREE

DRAWING COMPETITION

The date for the State Drawing Competition was fixed. Chedo had been chosen to represent her school after she emerged the best in the school's competition. During the competition at her school, pupils who had visual art talent were given the task to draw their favorite animal. Chedo drew a peacock. It was so beautiful that other competitors surrounded her and asked her to teach them how to draw such a beautiful peacock. Then all the participants were asked to present their drawings.

Chedo took the stage wearing a multicolored gown made of Ankara prints that her mother had made for her. She paired the dress with nice shoes, matching socks and her mother's jewelry.

"My name is Chedo Chike, I am seven years old. My favorite animal is a peacock. I like peacock because they are beautiful and like to display their flamboyant colours." She described the peacock while touching her presentation.

She continued, "The general name is peafowl, the male is peacock, while the female is peahen, but people are used to calling both peacocks."

She thanked the organizers for the opportunity to showcase her work and took a bow. Everyone clapped as she walked out of the stage after her brilliant presentation.

Her parents were filled with joy, seeing their baby girl made them proud. When she was announced the winner, she jumped up and danced all her favorite Nigerian dance, from traditional dance steps to contemporary ones like *Shaku-Skaku*, *Etighi*, *Alanta*, amongst others.

One week later, the head teacher of the school told her that she should prepare for the State Competition which would hold in Nnewi. The head teacher appointed Miss Taye, a class teacher, to take Chedo to the venue of the final competition.

The next morning, Miss Taye picked Chedo from her house where Chedo was already up and waiting, well dressed in yellow Ankara blouse, skirt, a matching ribbon to clip her hair, and a pair of pretty white shoes.

When they arrived, Chedo met beautiful people from all over the state. They were well dressed too. The competition was for children between the ages of six to twelve. Chedo saw that most of the participants were older and taller than her, so she whispered to her teacher, "They are so big, are you sure I will win? I am scared of losing."

"Courage, my dear, don't be intimidated. Just do your best, be positive and always remember that you are already a winner."

Miss Taye led Chedo into the hall and the compère announced that the participants would be drawing a peacock. Chedo had drawn a peacock before, so she eagerly took her writing materials and drew a beautiful peacock.

In less than an hour, Chedo was done and she watched other contestants struggle to design the feathers of their peacocks. The judges went round to see what everyone drew. Some drew a bird that looked like a chicken, others drew an ostrich. It was only Chedo that drew a proper peacock that proudly flaunted its train.

She was announced the winner and called to the stage to give a vote of thanks. Chedo was not prepared for the speech, so her teacher told her to go up the stage with a smile, and thank everyone including the organizers, her parents, teachers and other participants.

Chedo did just as she was told. She climbed up, took a microphone and spoke, "Good day everyone. I would like to thank the organizers for this event. I want to thank my parents, teachers and friends for supporting me. To other participants, I want to let you all know that you are all winners."

This speech made everyone clap really hard and Chedo left the stage when the ovation was loudest.

CHAPTER FOUR

EKA PLOTS AGAIN

The news of Chedo winning the state competition spread fast all over her town. Her parents had a surprise party for her.

Many parents changed their children's school to the school Chedo was attending because they believed the school would make their children smarter.

Eka and her friends did not like how everyone was praising Chedo but they decided to come up with a plan that will dim her shine.

"Chedo goes home alone, we can look for her trouble on her way home," Titi suggested.

"Oh yes, I also observed Kay has been absent from school so she will have no one to support her," Dera said.

"I am tired of everyday, Chedo, Chedo, Chedo, like she is the only one in this school." Eka complained.

The girls waited till afternoon when they saw Chedo going home. They approached her and threw a stone at her. Chedo missed her step and fell to the ground.

When they saw that she had fallen to the ground, they immediately ran to her. "You can win all the competitions in the world but you hand will still remain ugly," Eka said.

All the other girls laughed at her.

Those words struck Chedo and stung her badly.

She wondered why God created her with a big birthmark in an obvious place that everyone will see and laugh at.

She went home sad and on seeing her, her mother asked, "Che-Che, you look so sad. What happened?" Chizoba drew her daughter closer as she spoke.

"I hate my hand and this thing on it." She pointed at her birthmark. "I want my hand to be like others, Eka and her friends are laughing at me that my hand is ugly," Chedo said, tears dropping down her cheeks.

"Oh my child, how can you hate the same hand you have used to draw? Your birthmarks are unique, do not allow people's words break you."

Her mother's words gave her some comfort, but deep down, Chedo began to plot how to remove the birthmark.

CHAPTER FIVE

THE MAGICAL CREAM

Chedo continued to desire perfect arms. She imagined having hands like those of her friends, and people no longer mocking her.

Her neighbour, Mr James, was a close family member. Mr James had a store where he sold bleaching creams. He started the business when he realized that most people wanted a fairer skin tone. He made so much money from the business that he'd started building a magnificent house.

He had overheard Chedo cry about her birthmarks several times. One Sunday morning, he visited Chedo and her parents. Chedo's mother was a great cook and enjoyed cooking for friends and family.

"Chizoba, can you please make me rice and that unique stew you make?" Mr James asked.

"Oh you mean Ofe Akwu?" Chizoba asked.

"Yes please, I like the taste and aroma." Mr James replied in a happy tone. He knew that Chizoba would not say no to his request.

Chizoba went into the kitchen to prepare the delicious meal Mr James requested.

When he realised that she was no longer in the sitting room, Mr James went close to Chedo to speak with her.

Chedo was drawing when she turned back to see who had tapped her shoulder.

"Hello Che-Che, that is a beautiful work of art, you draw so well, congratulations on all of your achievements."

"Thank you sir," Chedo replied with a beautiful smile. People praise Chedo's gift so well and she always thanked them with a beautiful smile just as her mother taught her.

"I have a solution that will remove your scar overnight, so that you can be perfect like your friends," Mr James said.

"Wow! Please, can you give it to me? I want my hands to be fine so that my friends can stop laughing at me," Chedo cried.

"It is okay, you don't have to cry. It cost N1,000,000," Mr James said.

"What?" Chedo shouted and left her mouth wide open.

"Ssshhh, reduce your voice, we don't want your mummy to hear us. It passes several stages of production in different countries. It is made from elephant tusks and ostrich eggs. That is why it so expensive. Just go into the room and bring one of your mother's gold jewelry for me. She is in the kitchen and will not know. Run quickly," he said.

Chedo looked around to be sure her mother was not looking at them. She peeped in the kitchen and saw her mother pounding palm kernel in the mortar to make the soup Mr James requested.

Then she quickly went to her mother's jewelry box and brought one of her mother's necklaces.

"I will give him this, Mum does not wear this one, maybe she just does not like it," Chedo said.

She ran to Mr James and gave him the necklace. "Good girl, I will get you the magic cream that will remove your birthmarks. Let me eat this meal your mother is making for me first," he said.

"What are you two talking about? James, come over to the table to eat lunch, your food is ready," Chizoba said.

Mr James went to dining and ate the food fast, like someone who had not eaten for a year. His mouth was making loud sounds as he chewed his food, while his cutleries were making annoying clanging sounds. This made Chedo and her mother look at each other, wondering why he was eating this way.

"This food is so delicious, you are an excellent cook, Chizoba," he said, while coughing because the pepper in the food was choking him.

"Have water, don't talk while eating, and take it easy, the food is not running away, I will give you extra if this is not enough for you." Chizoba did not finish talking when Mr James interrupted.

"Yes, yes, please give me extra," he said.

"Ah, but you have not finished eating this, how do you know you will want more if you don't finish this first? Mum, is he a glutton?" Chedo asked.

"I am not a glutton, young girl. I just like good food. Everybody does," Mr James replied.

Chizoba and Chedo could not eat with Mr James on the same table because of his bad table manners, so they went to the sitting room to watch a movie.

Mr James ate two more plates and went home tired.

The next day, he came to Chedo's window and sneaked the cream to her as planned. He whispered to her, the instructions on how to use it.

Chedo was so happy, she had her bath and used the cream.

CHAPTER SIX

SIDE EFFECTS

C hedo used the magic cream Mr James gave her. She used it all the time because she wanted the mark to vanish quickly.

She also noticed that her skin was peeling off, but she thought the spot would peel off and her skin will get better afterwards.

It was her father's birthday, so Chedo and Chizoba planned a surprised party for Nonso. They could not invite family and friend because there was a pandemic and they did not want the virus, Covid-19, to spread.

Chizoba bought a green sleeveless dress for Chedo to wear for the family party. Chedo loved sleeveless dresses. After wearing her new gown, Chedo used a scarf to wrap her hands.

"Come closer, Chedo. Is that a scarf you are using to cover your hands, and why? You always liked sleeveless dresses," Chizoba said.

Chizoba went close to Chedo and removed the scarf. "Ah, what happened to you? When did this happen? Why did you not tell me?" Chizoba shouted.

"I didn't like my birthmark, so Mr James gave me a cream that would remove the mark, but now it gave me wounds and my skin started peeling," Chedo said.

"But I told you that you are perfect and should ignore people mocking your birthmark!"

Chizoba was so worried about her daughter's health, she called Nonso and they went to the hospital.

When they got the hospital, they saw Doctor Ken. He liked Chedo a lot because she was very smart.

"What brings you to my office today, and why are you and your daughter crying?" Doctor Ken asked.

Chizoba told him everything and he quickly ran some tests.

"That cream was very harsh on her skin, it's good that you came on time, you have to stop using it, otherwise, it can lead to cancer," Dr James said.

They went back home and Chedo went to rest.

While Chedo was resting, Chizoba and Nonso went to Mr James's house. They were angry at him for deceiving their daughter.

When they knocked on their door, Mrs James opened the door. Immediately they were ushered in, Chizoba noticed that Mrs James was wearing her necklace. The necklace was a gift from Chizoba's mum.

"Good evening, is your husband in? By the way, what is my necklace doing on your neck?" she asked.

Mr James was entering the living room from his room, he wanted to hide when he realized that Chedo's parents were there to see him, but Nonso saw him.

"You are welcome. Can you please sit down?" Mr James said.

"No, tell us what you gave our daughter to apply on her hand, and what is my wife's necklace doing on your wife's neck?" Nonso asked.

"Erm…Erm, she wanted me to give her a cream that will make her birthmark disappear, and she could not afford it, so I gave her the cream in exchange for the necklace," Mr James spoke, while looking away from them because he was scared.

"When did this happen? Don't you know that she is a child?" Chedo said.

"I am very sorry, it was the day you cooked for me," James responded.

This only made Chizoba angrier. She was sad that while she was cooking to make him happy, he was deceiving her daughter. She decided that she will be more careful about who she left her daughter with next time.

Chizoba collected her necklace and they left Mr James house.

Mr James was scared, he did not know what the next plan of Chedo's parents would be, so he convinced his wife to run away with him. He was afraid that he might be arrested by the police and spend time in jail.

"What will happen to our house rent? Have you forgotten that we just paid a year rent yesterday? How about our properties? What will we do to all we have?" Mrs James asked.

"It is better I lose everything than lose my freedom, I have just committed a serious crime," he responded.

They packed a few clothes and left everything else.

Meanwhile, when they got home, Chizoba went close to Chedo and touched her head to feel her temperature. She was a bit warm.

"You will be fine, my child."

"Thank you, Mum, for caring for me. I am sorry for everything."

"Now repeat after me," Chizoba urged her daughter. "My birthmark and my gift, they are different parts of me, and I love them both."

Chedo said the words and then her mother told her to say it ten times until the words became unforgettable to her.

"Every morning when you wake up, we will say this."

"Please, give me my board, I want to draw so that I will feel better."

Chizoba gave Chedo the board and she tried to draw, but something bad happened that made Chedo cry.

Her hand hurt so bad, it had become swollen because of the cream. She had big boils that touched the board when she drew and it made her feel so much pain. For the first time ever, Chedo could not draw and she started crying.

Her mother consoled her and told her to be patient until the wounds heal. This did not stop Chedo from crying. She was afraid that she would lose her gift and she would not be able to draw again. There was an art display coming up and she wanted to participate to showcase her work and it was just a week away.

CHAPTER SEVEN

GIFT AND APPRECIATION

Chedo could not go to school for a week because the doctors told her that exposing the wounds might lead to infections.

She also tried to draw but it was difficult and painful. Her arm was wrapped with the bandage. She missed drawing so much that she regretted ever trying to remove her birthmark.

Chedo was with her aunt and parents when Mrs Mary visited. Chedo missed her teacher so much that she ran to give her a hug.

"Mrs Mary, I am so happy to see you, I have been worried that I can't participate in the art exhibition because each time I try to draw, my hand hurts so much," Chedo said.

"Don't worry Chedo, if you do not participate in this exhibition, there will be others, just take your medicine and stop being worried." Mrs Mary replied.

At this time, Chizoba walked in and shouted, "Please tell her. She does not like to take her medicine."

Mrs Mary held Chedo's hands and told her to make a promise that she will take her medication.

"You can't get better if you don't take your medications," she said.

Chedo made a promise that she will take her medications.

Mrs Mary bought her many fruits, like bananas, oranges, apples, pineapple and mangoes.

They were fresh and colourful. When Chedo saw them, she became so happy and thanked her favorite teacher.

The teacher left after telling Chedo to attend the inter-house sport competition that will take place on Saturday.

Chedo was happy because inter-house sport events were always fun. Although she was not good at sports, she enjoyed watching her best friend, Kay, and other pupils participating.

When Mrs Mary left, Chedo called her mum and said to her: "I have learnt to appreciate everything about my body. I hope that these wounds heal and my birthmark returns, so that I can continue drawing. If anybody laughs at me, I will just ignore because they don't know any better."

"Good, I am happy you have realised how beautiful you are. There is a reason it is called Mburu pụta ụwa in Igbo, which is our language. This means, you came into world with it, truly my child, you are special."

Chedo smiled as her mother spoke to her.

"I have an idea," Chizoba said.

Chizoba went to her room, used a marker to paint her hand like Chedo's hand, and showed it to Chedo.

"I wished I could draw like you," Chizoba said.

Chedo was happy to see her mother desiring her birthmark and both of them laughed so hard when her mother tried to draw a car but it ended up looking like a house.

CHAPTER EIGHT

EKA'S SECRET

It was the day of the inter-house sport competition. The school surrounding was beautifully decorated. All the children wore colourful sport uniforms which indicated the houses they belonged to. The houses were named with colours. There was a Blue House, a Red House, a Yellow House and a White House. Parents also attended to cheer their children.

As Chedo walked in with her yellow sportswear, her classmates who had missed her ran towards her and gave her a hug.

Immediately after, they went to the field to participate in the inter-house sport competition.

Eka was a great athlete. She was also in yellow house just like Chedo. She represented her house every year in the 100 meters race and she always won.

This time, she took her space, confident that she will come first and take the Gold medal. She was winning when something happened. One of the athletes kicked her leg and she fell to the ground.

As she fell, other pupils ran towards her, including Chedo. The breeze blew Eka's shirt and everyone saw her big birthmark on her stomach.

"Wow! Look at that. Eka has a big mark on her stomach," one of the girls shouted.

The sport officials help her stand up and gave her glucose to drink.

One of the students asked, "Is it a birthmark?"

Chedo, Kay and Eka's friends were all surprised that Eka had a birthmark but was always mocking Chedo's.

Eka started crying that everyone has seen her birthmark.

"I am sorry for laughing at you," she apologised to Chedo.

"It is okay, be proud of yourself. I say this every morning, my mum taught me:

My birthmark and my gift,

They are different parts of me,

And I love them both," Chedo said.

Eka repeated it. Eka was surprised at Chedo's confidence and she learnt not to make fun of anybody ever again.

CHAPTER NINE

THE ART EXHIBITION

Three days to the exhibition, Chedo visited the doctor and the bandage was removed. The wounds were healing well and the doctor told her that she could continue drawing.

Dr Ken was impressed with how fast Chedo's wounds had healed. "I know that Children's wounds heal fast, but I am really impressed with yours, I can see you took your medicine."

After the doctor's appointment, she ran home and began to draw. She liked drawing animals, so she drew a Zebra, a Rabbit and her other favourite animals.

Her father printed them ahead of the exhibition.

On the day of the art exhibition, her father took her to the venue and helped her display her drawings.

People came from all over to see the arts exhibited that day. Those who saw Chedo's works were marvelled that a 7-year-old was that talented.

Mr Obi , the art collector, walked past and saw Chedo's work, he was impressed and bought everything from her stand. Mr Obi informed Chedo and her father that there was scholarship up to university level for the youngest artist.

When the exhibition ended and it was confirmed that Chedo was the youngest, the gift was given to her and she was awarded the scholarship.

People at the exhibition took pictures of her while she smiled cheerfully.

When Chedo and her parents got home, they told their relatives the good news and Chedo thanked her parents for raising her to be confident. She told them that she loved her birthmark even more and would never try to remove it again.

"Chedo, will you not go for surgery to remove the birthmark?" her mother teased.

"Oh no," she replied laughing. "Maybe this time, my hand will be cut off entirely and I will not be able to draw."

They laughed together.

Chedo grew up to become a successful artist and a role model to children.

Get other interesting titles from the author here:

www.chibuzorazubuike.com

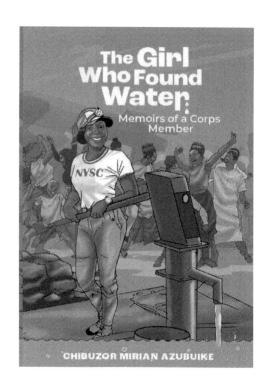

The Girl Who Found Water.

Made in the USA
Columbia, SC
29 September 2021

46406258R00043